ROSEMARY WELLS

Max Cleans Up

VIKING

VIKING
Published by the Penguin Group
Penguin Putnam Books for Young Readers, 345 Hudson Street,
New York, New York 10014, U.S.A.

Penguin Books Ltd, Registered Offices: Harmondsworth, Middlesex, England

First published in 2000 by Viking, a division of Penguin Putnam
Books for Young Readers.

10   9   8   7   6   5   4   3   2   1

LIBRARY OF CONGRESS CATALOGING-IN-PUBLICATION DATA
Wells, Rosemary.
Max cleans up / by Rosemary Wells.
        p.   cm.
Summary: Max's big sister Ruby is determined to help him clean up his
messy room, but he keeps rescuing things that she wants to throw away.
ISBN 0-670-89218-1 (hc)
[1. Orderliness—Fiction. 2. Brothers and sisters—Fiction.
3. Toddlers—Fiction. 4. Rabbits—Fiction.] I. Title.
PZ7.W46843 Mart 2000 [E]—dc21 99-462098

Printed in Hong Kong • Set in Minister

The art was created using ink, watercolors, rubber stamps, gouache, markers,
color pencils, pastels, string, cotton, rubber ants, cloth, bird gravel, silver foil,
a glue gun, feathers, fabric paint, and Miracle Bubbles.

Max parked his Popsicle where no one would find it.

Then he pushed the up-and-over button on his
brand new Power City Rocker Crusher dump truck.

"Max," said Max's sister, Ruby, "it's time to clean up!"

"Your dump truck goes back in the sandbox."

When Ruby wasn't looking, Max emptied the dump truck into his pocket.

Just then, Ruby stepped on something sticky.
It was a tube of Miracle Bubbles.

"Into the rubbish, Max," said Ruby.

But Max squeezed the rest of the Miracle Bubbles into his pocket, too.

"Your ant farm ants have escaped, Max," said Ruby.
"Back home they go!"

But Max let the ants run into his pocket instead
of into the ant farm.

"Max," said Ruby, "something's in your underwear drawer that should not be there."

"This Easter egg is from last year, Max," said Ruby.
"Into the trash bucket it goes!"

But Max stuffed the egg into his pocket.
"What is oozing out from under your closet door,
Max?" asked Ruby.

Max knew Ruby would find a reason to throw out his
Popsicle. She might even throw out his Quack-Quack Duck.

They both just fit in his pocket.

"Max," said Ruby, "your pillow is in your toy chest and your toys are in your bed."

Max rescued his very favorite piece of Gum-on-a-
String from the bottom of his bug box.
"Spit it out, Max!" said Ruby.

Ruby put all the toys in the toy chest.

She lined up the Santas

and the dolls.

The sneakers went into Max's closet and the windup bugs went into the bug box.

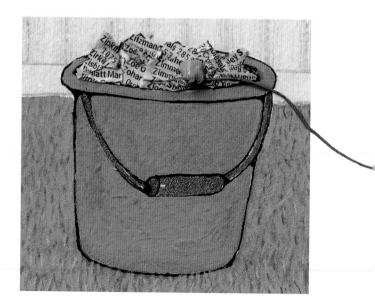

Max saved the gum in his pocket.

"Look, Max!" said Ruby. "Your room is completely organized. There is a place for everything and everything is in its place."

"Max," Ruby asked, "what is in your pocket?"

"Everything!" said Max.